THE FISHERMAN
AND HIS WIFE

THE FISHERMAN

illustrated by **Margot Tomes**

AND *HIS WIFE*

Retold from the Brothers Grimm
by **John Warren Stewig**

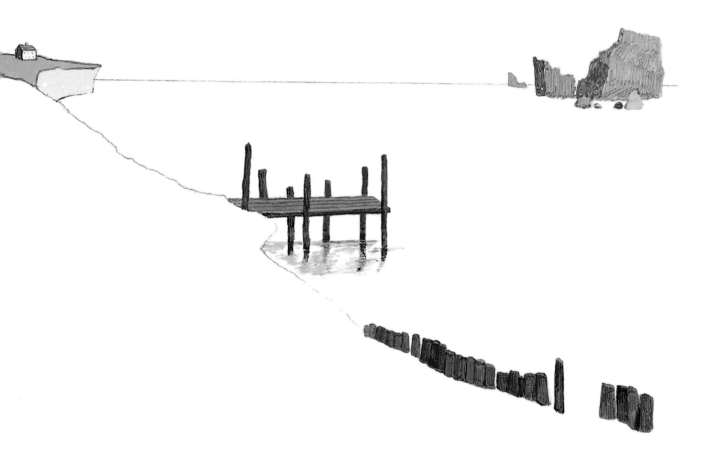

Holiday House / New York

Library of Congress Cataloging-in-Publication Data
Stewig, John W.
The fisherman and his wife/retold by John Warren Stewig;
illustrated by Margot Tomes. — 1st ed.
p.   cm.
Summary: The fisherman's greedy wife is never satisfied with the
wishes granted her by an enchanted fish.
[1. Fairy tales. 2. Folklore—Germany.]   I. Tomes, Margot, ill.
II. Title.
PZ8.S64Fi 1988   398.2—dc19   [E]   88-1698 CIP AC
ISBN 0-8234-0714-4

For R.D.B.

J.W.S.

To my Mississippi cousin,
Jane Carr Jameson

M.T.

There was once a poor fisherman and his wife who lived in a miserable hovel close by the sea. All would have been well, except for one thing. The fisherman had married a woman who daily regretted he was so ill-equipped to provide for her wants.

Despite this, life fell into a comfortable pattern of making do and scraping by. Each morning the fisherman gathered up his poles, picked up his fishing basket, and trudged across the fields to the side of the sea. There he spent his day baiting his hook, dropping his line, and watching for fish in the clear water. Meanwhile, his wife stayed home, minding the house and regretting she had married a man so easily satisfied with his lot.

Now this particular day began much as any other. The fisherman and his wife breakfasted on a meager meal of bread and fish. Then the fisherman trudged across the fields to the side of the sea, where he spent the morning watching for fish. Around midday, he felt a strong tug on his line. He quickly pulled it in, and was amazed to see a fine flounder instead of the scrawny carp he usually caught. The flounder further amazed the fisherman by speaking.

"Oh, fisherman, please set me free. I am not what I appear to be. Rather, I am a prince imprisoned in this shape by evil magic. Since I am man, not fish, I would be tough and stringy, not good to eat. Therefore, fisherman, please release me, and you shall have my gratitude."

Now the fisherman was a just man and so he carefully removed the hook and tossed the fish back into the water.

"Fisherman, you have my undying thanks," said the flounder as he flipped his tail and swam away, leaving a long streak of blood behind him.

The fisherman spent the rest of the afternoon peacefully enough, and when the sun had left the sky, he went home with his usual catch of scrawny carp.

The fisherman and his wife were almost finished with their supper when the wife asked, "What happened today, good husband?" When he told her of his encounter with the flounder, she railed, "You silly fool! Go back to the flounder and demand that he grant you a wish. He owes you one for sparing his life."

The poor fisherman looked confused. "But wife, what would I wish for?" he asked. "We have food on our table and a roof over our heads, so what more do we need?"

"What more do we need!" his wife exclaimed indignantly. "I'll tell you what we need . . ." and her voice softened as she began to dream. "I'll have, let me see . . . yes, I'll have a cottage, set about with a white picket fence and hollyhocks growing at the entryway." So she said in a determined voice:

> Go now, good husband
> to the fish.
> And tell him loudly
> what I wish.

Her husband protested:

> Oh, please, good woman
> do not ask
> That I begin
> this awful task.

But nothing would stop her, the woman was determined. So the hapless fisherman had no choice but to trudge back across the fields to the side of the sea. When he got there, he noticed the water was green and yellow, and not nearly so clear as before.

Nonetheless, being more frightened of his wife than of the flounder, the fisherman planted his heels firmly in the sand and in a loud voice sang out:

> Oh man, oh man, if man you be,
> Or flounder, flounder in the sea.
> Such a tiresome wife I've got.
> For she wants what I do not.

The flounder instantly appeared and asked the fisherman what he wanted. When the fisherman related his wife's demand, the flounder replied, "So it is asked, so it is given."

The fisherman was astonished when he returned home and found his wife waiting in the doorway of a tidy, small cottage, surrounded by a white picket fence, and with hollyhocks growing at the entryway. The house itself was a delight. There was a fireplace in the living room, a kitchen furnished with all manner of cooking utensils, and a snug pantry laden with unusual foods. Upstairs a cozy bedroom was lighted by a dormer window. When the fisherman looked out, he saw a garden filled with vegetables and fruits. Beside the garden was a fowl yard, crowded with ducks, geese, and chickens.

As the couple settled into their bed for the night, the fisherman said, "And now, wife, we can rest content." But his wife replied, "We'll see, husband, we'll see."

Things went well for ten days or a fortnight, until one day the wife said, "See here, husband, this cottage is really too small. It gives me no elbowroom. I'll tell you what we need . . ." and her voice softened as she began to dream. "I'll have a castle—a large stone castle, set at the end of a driveway bordered with olive trees. It should have rooms filled with crystal chandeliers, and furniture made of rare and beautiful wood." Then she went on, in a determined voice:

> Go now, good husband
> to the fish.
> And tell him loudly
> what I wish.

Her husband protested:

> Oh, please, good woman
> do not ask
> That I begin
> this awful task.

But there was no avoiding it: the woman was insistent. So the dauntless fisherman trudged back across the fields to the side of the sea.

When he got there, he noticed the water was still smooth but no longer green and yellow as before. Instead it was purple and blue and thick. Nonetheless the fisherman, more afraid of his wife than of the flounder, planted his heels firmly in the sand, and in a loud voice sang out:

> Oh man, oh man, if man you be,
> Or flounder, flounder in the sea.
> Such a tiresome wife I've got.
> For she wants what I do not.

At that instant the flounder appeared and asked curtly what the fisherman wanted. When the fisherman finished relating his wife's demand, the flounder replied, "So it is asked, so it is given."

The fisherman's jaw dropped when he returned home and found his wife waiting in the doorway of a stone castle, set at the end of a driveway shaded by large olive trees. Inside, servants led the fisherman and his wife through many stone hallways and up and down many stone staircases.

Everywhere they looked there were doors. Each opened onto a room more beautiful than the last, with furniture of rare wood carved in intricate shapes and upholstered in the finest fabric.

There were crystal chandeliers and cushioned carpets. All the tables were laid with the best of food and wine. Outside the castle, surrounding the courtyard, were stables for the animals and coach houses for the carriages. The gardens, trimmed, pruned, and weeded to perfection, stretched fully half a mile. Flowers and fruits and vegetables grew everywhere.

When they went to bed that night, the fisherman said, "And now, wife, we can rest content." But all she replied was, "We'll see, husband, we'll see."

The next morning, just as the first ray of the sun touched the stone sill of their bedroom window, the fisherman's wife awakened.

"Come here, husband," she said, "for I have made a decision." Her husband hesitated, but complied. "It is no good," she declared, "to have a beautiful castle without ruling the land it overlooks. So go to the flounder and tell him that . . . we should be king over all the lands."

"Wife," he responded, "what should we be king for? I don't want to be king."

"Well, I *do* want to be king, so go to your flounder and tell him what I have decided. I shall be king over all the lands I can see."

Now her husband, in addition to being afraid to return to the flounder, was put out with his wife for her wish. So he summoned his courage and protested:

> Oh, please, good woman
> > do not ask
> That I begin
> > this awful task.

But she was not to be refused, and insisted:

> Go now, good husband
> > to the fish.
> And tell him loudly
> > what I wish.

So there was nothing to do but for the husband to trudge back across the fields to the side of the sea. When he got there he noticed the sea was dark gray and gave off a pungent odor.

But, being more afraid of his wife than of the flounder, the fisherman planted his heels in the sand by the side of the sea, and in a loud voice sang out:

> Oh man, oh man, if man you be,
> Or flounder, flounder in the sea.
> Such a tiresome wife I've got.
> For she wants what I do not.

At that moment, the flounder appeared and briskly commanded the fisherman to state what he wanted. When the fisherman had relayed his wife's demand, the flounder replied, "So it is asked, so it is given."

The fisherman's eyes opened wide when he returned home, for a tall stone wall had appeared around the castle, and when he looked through the iron gates, he could see that the castle was far grander than the one he'd left, and was surrounded by oak trees. At each of the castle's four corners stood a tower, and in front of the doorway stood a sentry in a red velvet coat. The fisherman's wife was nowhere to be seen, but one of the footmen led him to the throne room. Its doors were fully twice as tall as the fisherman, and on each side were pillars of elaborately carved marble. When the doors were thrown open, the fisherman saw that a regal red carpet led to the throne. He was amazed when he saw his wife, arrayed in cloth of gold, sitting upon the throne. She had a gold crown studded with jewels on her head, and motioned him to approach.

"So you see, husband, I am king," said the fisherman's wife.

"And now, wife, we can rest content," the fisherman replied hopefully.

"We'll see, husband, we'll see," the king responded.

Early the next morning the fisherman was awakened by a sharp rapping on his door. It was a sentry summoning him to the throne room, for his wife had awakened early and gone directly there.

"What do you want, wife?" the fisherman asked wearily. "Husband," his wife responded, "since I am so capable as king over all the lands I can see, I shall be emperor over all the lands I cannot see."

By this time the husband knew it was futile to argue, so when the king commanded:

> Go now, good husband
>   to the fish.
> And tell him loudly
>   what I wish,

the husband could do nothing but feebly protest:

> Oh, please, good woman
>   do not ask
> That I begin
>   this awful task.

The luckless fisherman trudged across the fields to the side of the sea. When he got there he saw that the water was black and thick, and the foam flew up where the waves crashed against the rocks.

However, being less frightened of the flounder than of his wife, he planted his heels in the sand and sang out in a loud voice:

> Oh man, oh man, if man you be,
> Or flounder, flounder in the sea.
> Such a tiresome wife I've got.
> For she wants what I do not.

At that moment the flounder appeared and demanded to know what the fisherman wanted. When the fisherman had finished, the flounder snapped, "So it is asked, so it is given."

This time when the fisherman approached the castle, he was almost blinded by the glint of the sun on the alabaster which adorned the walls. At the side of the doors were trumpeters and drummers to announce the emperor's guests. Inside, a sentry led the fisherman up one stone hallway and down the next to the throne room.

When the doors were opened, the fisherman saw that the room was crowded with nobility dressed in an amazing array of silks and satins, paying homage to the emperor. And there, on the other side of a room so huge that one could scarcely see the far wall, sat his wife. Her throne was covered with beaten gold and studded with precious stones. And she had on a gold crown, three tiers high, topped with a ruby as big as an egg.

The sentry motioned the fisherman to approach the royal throne, and so he did, with eyes cast down. His wife said, pleasantly enough, "Well, husband, while you were gone the flounder made me emperor. As you can see, I do it well."

"Yes, and now wife, we can rest content."

"Not yet husband, not yet," his wife replied.

"Why, wife," the fisherman said, "now that you are emperor, there is nothing left to be."

"Oh, but husband, there is. Since I am such a capable emperor, next I shall be Pope."

The husband was aghast, and protested:

> Oh, please, good woman
>   do not ask
> That I begin
>   this awful task.

But he knew in his heart it would do no good, so he was
not surprised to hear her respond:

> Go now, good husband
>> to the fish
> And tell him loudly
>> what I wish.

The woman was determined, so the fisherman had no
choice but to trudge back across the fields to the side of the
sea. When he got there, the sky was as black and churning as
the water. A great wind bent the trees almost to the ground,
and its sound mingled with the roaring of the sea that crashed
and splashed against the rocks.

The fisherman, to the end more afraid of his wife than of the flounder, planted his heels firmly in the sand, and in a loud voice sang out:

> Oh man, oh man, if man you be,
> Or flounder, flounder in the sea.
> Such a tiresome wife I've got.
> For she wants what I do not.

Almost before he has finished, the flounder appeared and commanded: "Speak, fisherman." When the fisherman had finished telling of his wife's demand, the flounder responded, "So it is asked, so it is given."

Then the fisherman went home. When he got there he saw a large church surrounded by palaces. Outside, a crowd of people had gathered, but he pushed his way through. Inside, the church was lit by more candles than anyone could count. His wife was dressed in golden cloth, sitting on a much higher throne than before, and she wore on her head three golden crowns, one on top of the other. Kneeling before her, waiting their turn to kiss her shoe, were all the other kings and emperors.

"Wife," said the fisherman, "are you Pope now?"

"Yes," she said, "I am Pope."

"Well, wife, now we can rest content," the fisherman replied hopefully.

"We'll see, husband, we'll see," the Pope replied.

The next morning the poor fisherman was awakened early, summoned by one of his wife's attendants. He had slept soundly because he had done a great deal of work the previous day. But his wife had tossed and turned restlessly all night, planning what she could still become. When the first rays of the sun crept across her windowsill, the idea came to her. "I have it! I shall make the sun and moon rise and set."

The poor fisherman was still half asleep when he stumbled into the Pope's bedroom. He could not believe what she told him.

"What did you say, wife?"

"I shall never have a quiet moment until I can make the sun and moon rise and set. Go to your fish, and tell him I will be like unto God."

The fisherman summoned up his courage and protested:

> Oh, please, good woman
>   Do not ask
> That I begin
>   this awful task.

But she was determined to have her way, and insisted:

> Go now, good husband
>   to the fish.
> And tell him loudly
>   what I wish.

The fisherman shuddered, but the determined look in her
eye told him he had no choice but to return to the fish.

As he trudged across the fields to the side of the sea, the fisherman was nearly bent double by the howling wind. Trees and houses toppled over, the very mountains trembled, and the sky was pitch black. The sea crashed against the rocks, sending black waves as tall as buildings splashing over the land.

The fisherman, more afraid of his wife than he was of the flounder, planted his heels firmly in the sand. In a loud voice—which he could not himself hear because of the thunder—he sang out:

Oh man, oh man, if man you be,
Or flounder, flounder in the sea.
Such a tiresome wife I've got.
For she wants what I do not.

"Well, what does she want now?" asked the flounder.
"Alas," replied the fisherman, "she wants to be like unto God." To which the flounder responded, "Go home. She shall have what she deserves."

And when the fisherman returned home, he found his wife in their miserable little hovel.